Brewl

The existence of Nothing

Introduction

"Before all things there was nothing, and so nothing alone was"

Book one

"Nothingness"

Verse 1

In the beginning there was nothing, and it was alone, and it was void of shape or substance for no shapes nor substances yet existed, and it was nameless, for names are given and no one yet lived to give it a name, it lived nowhere, for there was yet to be anywhere to live, it felt nothing, ate nothing and thought nothing, for it was the very existence of nothingness, unaffected by time yet present throughout all time, nothing, alone, was.

Verse 2

Absent of light, it was pitch black, and so, this the pitch black darkness was the light, timeless, it became time itself, motionless, it became motion and began the flow of time, weightless, yet bearing the weight of all existence, it became weight itself, with no form nor shape, it became fluid, lacking warmth, it became cold, so cold that it became hot, with no beginning, there would be no end to it, without life, it was death, and without death, it was life, empty, it became something, for to be empty one must first be able to contain, and thus nothing became an infinite black sea.

Verse 3

An endless black sea of nothingness, containing the very essence of existence, spanning across infinity, nothing truly existed, and so it did, for to have nothing exist means nothing must first exist, thus the infinite black sea was existence itself.

Verse 4

What is water? How can we calculate all that goes into a single drop of water? How small could a single drop of water become if a drop was taken from a drop? Then another from another, and another from another, over and over, drop from drop, before you realize water is only the accumulation of what makes it up, it has no form, no size, weight or temperature, water truly is the closest thing to nothing, which is why creation took the form of a sea, an ocean of creative and destructive energy, merging to make up the endless black waters.

Verse 5

These two opposing energies would come to be known as, "Ven, the element of destruction itself, capable of reducing anything it comes in contact with into nothingness, air, water, fire, earth and even light itself, anything that exist can be returned to nothing" and "Ni, the element of creation itself, capable of replicating and giving life and form to anything it comes in contact with including thoughts, anything can exist since nothing does" together Ven and Ni form NiVen which is the balance that keeps the endless sea stable, they can not exist without each other for they are one and the same, which is proof of the existence of nothing.

Verse 6

The prophet of prophets, the child known as Niko Brel found himself drowning within the infinite black sea, surrounded and within the all

of nothingness, only nothing
knows why he was chosen,
because nothing alone chose
him, pulled from his time into
the beginning of time, he
would give nothing a name.
Verse 7

A gift for a gift, in exchange
for his name nothing agreed
to give the boy a gift, the
ability to see Brewl, to see the
history of all things, the true
bible, unlike other Knowa
who can only see glimpses of
Brewl, Niko Brel would be
able to see it all, through all
times, at all times, and he
would chronicle this history

and be the author of Brewl, which is why it was named after him.

Verse 8

Nikrolos would be the name of nothingness, the name of existence itself, father of fathers, creator of creators, the very existence of nothingness, after receiving his name from the child of prophecy, Nikrolos returned the child to his world making him an eternal constant in existence, like Nikrolos, Niko Brel would exist throughout all timelines and a form of

Niko Brel would exist throughout all worlds.

Verse 9

It was dark, Nikrolos received so much more than just a name from the child of prophecy, he received and understanding of everything he would create as well as how void his world was at the moment, and so he began to create.

Verse 10

Day 1, Nikrolos created balance by separating opposing forces, light from dark, heat from cold, Nikrolos created Noras, orbs of light to illuminate the infinite black sea, these Noras would act as funnels radiating NiVen within rays of light.

Day 2, Water and Light would be the food of the oldest living creature in existence, an eternal constant, a creature existing in all timelines known as Nozark, from a seed, this creature would grow in all directions, its size is infinite, vines, branches, roots rooted in eternity, fruit containing heavens, plants harboring worlds, and fungus imprisoning hells.

Day 3, Dregulus, if Nozark was created to create and maintain life, then Dregulus were created to destroy and consume that life, in order to maintain balance Nikrolos would create Dregulus, creatures of the infinite black sea as large as worlds and some even larger that would feed on Nozark and excrete Varlock, condensed mineral NiVen.

Day 4, The old ones,

centuries of Dregulus feeding on Nozark cultivated the perfect breeding ground for beings strong enough to defend themselves from the threat of the Dregulus scourge, thus Nikrolos created the Nags, divine beings with immense spiritual energy known as Nivenity, although smaller in stature compared to Dregulus, Nags spiritual Nivenity is on par if not greater in some cases then that of Dregulus.

Verse 14

Day 5, After centuries of waring with the Dregulus, the

Nags established territories that were protected from Dregulus attacks which allowed life to began to bloom on worlds under the protection of the Nags, Nikrolos created creatures of all types, shapes and sizes, but these creatures Nivenity would be weak due to the difference in heavens and earths, heavens are worlds within the fruit of Nozark where the air, light, food and water are filled with high concentrations of NiVen, where as earths on the other hand, air, light, food and water have significantly less concentrations of NiVen.

Day 6, Civilization, after centuries of Nags overseeing natural selection, watching animal and insect species come and go, Nikrolos created intelligent life forms capable of complex thought and the ability to form lasting bonds and tribal structures which lead to the rise of the first civilizations throughout the many earths of Nozark, the oldest civilization being the NiJaBre, named after the child of prophecy and direct ancestors of the child of prophecy the NiJaBre klan would become the apple of the eye of Nikrolos, a chosen people.

Day 7, after all Nikrolos created he decided it was time to rest and in his slumber he would create the afterlife, a dreamlike collective consciousness for the dead known as NiziN, this realm would connect all worlds and would be the beginning and end of all souls journeys, both mortal and immortal, everything comes from Nikrolos and in the end everything shall return to Nikrolos.

Verse 17

Nazeerah the Krowlock of Krowlocks, in the new age of Nags after centuries of internal wars as well as battles against the Dregulus, beings that were seemingly immortal began to die left and right, a power struggle ensued due to a lack of leadership, everyone wanted to rule yet none were worthy, and as the Nags warred in the heavens, civilizations warred on the earths, and so a Nag of war was born, forged in the flames of war the young Nazeerah was born to a noble klan of Nags known as the Kaneos, known for their skill in combat and their ability to control divine flames they were a mighty klan of Nags, yet their insatiable thirst for battle caused them to nearly war themselves to the brink of extinction, by the time Nazeerah was born he was merely one of a handful of living Kaneos klan members.

Verse 18

As centuries past Nazeerah grew from a child to a man and built up a great army of Nags from different klans with different abilities, this was much different from other leaders who mainly lead armies of Nags from their own klan, it would be this key difference along with Nazeerahs great might that would allow him to be victorious over his competition, and before he knew it Nazeerah was the Krowlock of Krowlocks ruler of rulers, the great lord Nag

of the heavens and his army
of Nags his royal Kounts.

Verse 19

After becoming Krowlock
Nazeerah set his sights on
and uninhabited heaven that
he and his Kounts would
make their Dominion and
below it an earth where he
would raise up a mighty
people, however this would
be the true test of his might
for this would be the first
time he would ever do battle
with a Dregulus, and in his
first battle with a Dregulus he
would be facing two
Dregulie, Leeriad the

destroyer and father of Drekans and his companion Bezoneer the devourer of worlds, after centuries of battle Nazeerah realized the best course of action would be to imprison these great beast in cages of eternal divine flames fueled by the will of Nazeerah himself.

Verse 20

The oldest and most advanced civilization of mortals known as the NiJaBre were able to travel throughout Nozark bringing their knowledge, culture and most of all their seed with them allowing them to populate many worlds over, Nazeerahs world was no exception, descendants of the great NiJaBre klan were all over Nazeerahs earth, and it would be from this bloodline Nazeerah would choose the seed for his mighty nation of people, a people who's stubbornness and foolishness would know no bounds and would lead them in and out of times of great power and prosperity as well as times of great suffering and pain, for like their great Nag Nazeerah they to are a people of fire, burning with great passion and talent and overflowing with potential, and like their great Nag they to are a young people who have not yet matured to their full potential, and the name of these hardheaded trouble makers would be Negarza, the children of the Nag.

Verse 21

In the old world when all people were of one people there was a man destined to be the father of nations, his name was Knowa and he was a great fisherman and ship builder, within the hierarchy of the NiJaBre klan knowa was insignificant and yet he was chosen to be the first prophet by the almighty Nikrolos.

Verse 22

A vision of a great storm is what he was shown, a flood that would swallow the world, hearing the news the elders and leaders of the NiJaBre klan weren't shocked, for they knew their Nyontifek advancements were to blame.

Verse 23

Using Nyince which is the study of nature and the natural world in order to understand the inner workings of the physical realm and reality, Nyontist were filled with and insatiable hunger for knowledge, for knowledge brought them that much closer to Nikrolos.

Verse 24

Two factions formed, one of Nyince who believed through knowledge and understanding they could reach the realm of Nikrolos and learn the secrets of all existence, and a faction of Nivenist that decided to merely live by faith and be one with nature and

Nivenity, of these two factions Knowa was a Nivenist.

The Nyontist among the NiJaBre had created machines capable of transporting them between worlds through Nozark itself, but this travel would mean a brief disruption of the earths Breya, a dome like veil separating the infinite black sea from the earth.

For fourteen months Knowa and his faction worked tirelessly to build a fleet of ships larger than any ships in history, great arks designed to carry nations of people and species of animals, these arks would become the cradle of all life on earth.

Verse 27

As the NiJaBre faction of Nyontist pierced the Breya veil to leave their earth the black rains began to fall, filled with raw unfiltered NiVen, a single drop of black sea water equivalent to and ocean of earth water this black rain would swallow the world in fourteen days, and filled with the elements of existence, this event would start off as a disaster yet in the end the earth would come back stronger than ever.

Verse 28

Fourteen decades, would be the time necessary for the earth to drain out the excess water and integrate the excess NiVen into itself, over the course of those many years living on the arks, many bloodlines were lost through great wars that took place, epic sea battles raged on along side the rising of great civilizations, mythical creatures evolved from the higher NiVen concentration within the earth, this water world was truly an age pirates could only dream of, an age known as Seviare, named after a great sea Nag Seviarus.

Verse 29

Seviare, the age of the sea, one hundred and forty years of mankind supporting its own existence as well as most animal existences on ships and wooden floating cities, seven nations born of the seed of Knowa would rule the seas, at the dawn of Seviare Knowa would take seven wives who would bare him seven sons, and these sons would be Vikrendor the world splitter, Negamureno the red rain, Kastigma the lightening current, Euphrea the forked tongue, Tankue the false smile, Kushemett the wise, and Kremenalle the wild, these seven sons would create seven nations named in their honor.

Verse 30

The end of the age of Seviare meant a race to carve up territories on the earth, the seven nations of knowa each took a continent for themselves while other smaller nations took islands as their territories.

Xkardem, a scene that influences nightmares, the infinite black sea ablaze, clouds of blood in the sky, the scent of death and rotting flesh, red oceans and continents made of dead bodies, these were just a few images seen by Philias a young Knowa born on the island of Kiliwa off the coast of Kremenalle, he was the first Knowa to prophesy about Xkardem, even though the NiJaBre klan found a krown with the name engraved on it many millennia earlier, this prophecy was seen as blasphemous and Philias and his family and friends were seen as Vermaya and rounded up nailed to a tree and burned alive.

Verse 32

The dying mother and the winged Jekon, for centuries man would war against a race of beings known as Jekons, who were known for their brutality even towards their own, one evening a

Knowa by the name Seyona
would prophesy the attack on
a Jekon girl by Jekon warriors
who would rape and leave
her for dead, enraged the girl
would seek out the cage of
Leeriad and sneak in to
acquire his seed, after laying
with the Dregulus she
became pregnant and seven
days later she died giving
birth to seven Drekans,
winged reptile like creatures
of Jekon size, with scales
harder than diamond, lava
for saliva and fire for breath,
these creatures with a hunger
for flesh would become the

greatest enemy of the Jekon race.

The last storm and Reny the clear skied fool, a young Knowa by the name Reny would try his best to warn his fellow villagers of a storm of burning rain that would set the earth on fire and turn the sky into ash, sadly for Reny he did not know this vision was of a distant future and what he thought was rain was actually a Varlock shower, he was label a fool and outcasted only to live to and old age and watch his people erased from the earth once the Varlock rains finally came.

Verse 34

To be a Knowa, to see and know things no one else does was confusing for most born with the ability, and for many telling others about these prophecies was a death sentence, and thus the start of Knowa killings began, a cult known as Sightenance was formed to hide the existence of Knowa and their prophecies while hunting, killing and removing their eyes in an attempt to control this power for themselves.

Verse 35

The hunting of Knowa by Sightenance forced people with the gift to hide their abilities and instead write these prophecies down anonymously for others to read, this was the turning point for religion, what was once oral traditions was now written skrolls full of information no normal person should know, the past, present and future as well as knowledge of other worlds and information about the great Nags, heavens and hells all written on skrolls known as Brewl.

Verse 36

Pages, or skrolls of Brewl were popping up in Krodaminions all over the world and Krowlocks were all but desperate to gain possession of them, he who could control Brewl could control the religions of the worlds, and so the page wars began, Krodaminions waged war against each other in order to unite the pages of Brewl into one book controlled by one Krowlock.

Verse 37

Xkardem, written by branding the information onto hides of human flesh and bound to a human tibia bone with human hair to form a book, the book of Xkardem was found in Hedaneya the Krodaminion of Grigreyar the bloody, a Krowlock known for his savagery, the Knowa who wrote it is unknown, the language it was written in is unknown, and everyone in Grigreyars Krodaminion, over ten thousand people were all found dead, Grigreyar included, even more shocking is they all took their own lives.

News of the book of Xkardem sent chills of fear throughout the world months after its discovery Grigreyars Krodaminion was left unoccupied out of fear that what happened could happen again, this made it the perfect location for runaway Xleva to hide out and over time build their ranks, angry at the world around them and both fearing and respecting the power of Xkardem that gave them a safe haven, the now

freed Xleva took the name
Xkars and devoted their
existence to seeing the rise of
Xkardem and the end of all
existence.
Verse 39
Many skrolls would be
written by unknown Knowa
who's names would be lost in
time yet their prophecies
would live on forever,
prophecies of mans triumph
over the mythical beast of
old, visions of distant futures
filled with unknown
technologies, the rise and fall
of Krowlocks, and the birth
of political structures that put

and end to the reign of Krowlocks in exchange for elected officials and modern governments, details on Nag bloodlines and klan structures, and most importantly prophecies about the coming child of the great lord Nag Nazeerah.

Verse 40

Religions based on the prophecies written about on the pages of Brewl began to take shape all over the world, this worship by humans for Nags caused many Nags to make themselves known to Pagestors, people who could decipher the pages of Brewl and act as a go between for humanity and Nags, although many were legitimate over time being a Pagestor became big business and frauds turned the title into a get rich quick scheme, it wouldn't be long before the Legalia cult infiltrated the Pagestor ranks and quickly made religious institutions another branch in their tree of power.

Verse 41

Altevo a young poet thrusted into madness by the visions of what he would see from his gift would end up writing many skrolls about different time periods all dealing with Xlevary, his nightmares plagued by images of people in chains, beaten and tortured to within inches of death and worked mercilessly until the point of a cruel miserable death would haunt him however it was his vision of what this practice would birth that truly terrified him, he wrote of the Xkars and how their numbers would grow and how they would recruit their fellow Xleva to fight towards the destruction of the world, and he foretold of a leader among the Xkars that would be born of both human and Nag blood his name would be Xlade and his blood would transform his army of human Xkars into an army of mythical creatures that feed on the pain and fear of their victims, over time people would forget Xkars origins only knowing the mythology of them as a creature of darkness.

Verse 42

Altevo believed his writings would change something, possibly put and end to Xlevary in order to stop the

future creation of a race of
creatures that would become
a threat to humanity, and yet
his writings did nothing, no
Krodaminion that practiced
Xlevary would part with their
Xlevas because of someones
nightmares, this would force
Altevo to speak out against
Xlevary and any Krowlocks
that practiced it, this caused
him to be marked for death,
he would be arrested, tried
and convicted and sentenced
to death by a thousand lashes
with a bladed whip.
Verse 43

A dry cold, an ash covered landscape covered in fossilized trees and plant life, bones of long dead creatures of all shapes and sizes, and the mold covered bodies of the dying slowly being consumed by the world around them, these are visions of hell, although many unknown Knowa have written about various different hells this hell was different, this vision was different, foretold by Maleki the crazed, a Knowa who's dream was to be a famous artist even though he lacked the raw talent, one day began painting works of art depicting scenes from hell, his greatest masterpiece would be a portrait of the birth of a child born in hell, the painting would be called NagFall.

Verse 44

The rise and fall of Krodaminions hinged on the possession of pages of Brewl, within them was information that helped civilizations advance far beyond their predecessors, Sekloth of the sand would prophesy of a great nation being built in a desert area of Kushemett, his tale described a people more advance than their rivals, with millions of Xlevas and riches beyond all others, led by Krowlocks said to be descended from the Nags, this Krodaminion would be known as Egyah.

Verse 45

The rise of the Kreatans, a race of beings born from Dregulus and Nag conception, these beings who were worshiped as Nags by the Jekon nations who were born from Kreatan and human conception, were imprisoned by Nazeerahs forefathers in a cage of ice below Vikrendor on earth, this vision was considered to be and end time event, thus on the words of Elios the Knowa who prophesied these events a rise in Jekon slayings began in hopes of avoiding the revival of their fallen Kreatans.

Verse 46

Mazeery, son of Xlevas in Egyah, his mother would put him in a basket and send him adrift in a river in hopes her son would avoid Xlevary, this act would land him at the feet of the wife of Egyahs Krowlock who would take him in as her own child and raise him in the capitol of Egyah in the castle of the great Krowlock Pharoshima.

Verse 47

Mazeery was raised like a Krow, groomed to one day be a Krowlock along side the Krowlocks son Pharoshem, the two young Krows grew up together as brothers, not by blood but by Nivenity.

Verse 48

On Mazeerys eighteenth birthday he would come across a Xleva girl who

claimed to know his mother, and told him he was born a Xleva, he swiftly dismissed the girl, in his heart he was Egyian but the girl believed him to be Negarza.
Verse 49

Mazeery questioned the Deva, wife of the Krowlock, about his birth parents, and she explained how she found him which matched the story of how his mother sent him adrift in the river as told to him by the Xleva girl, in that moment he knew the girls story was true.
Verse 50

Mazeery would flee Ramshemere the capitol of Egyah ashamed of his Xleva origins, for many years he would live amongst a village of Negarza people in the neighboring city of Koetza where he would learn about his peoples history, years would past and when Mazeery was twenty four he would have his first vision of the future.

Verse 51

The great lord Nag Nazeerah showed Mazeery images of Egyah in ruins, a sight that terrified and sadden him because of his love for the Krodaminion and family he grew up with, he was told by Nazeerah that Egyah would only be spared if his Negarza people were set free.

Mazeery returned home to the capitol in order to speak to the Krowlock, to his surprise Pharoshima had died a year earlier and Pharoshem was now Krowlock of Egyah, the brothers were both overjoyed to see each other although it was bitter sweet, their father was dead and Mazeery not being there for the funeral made things more than a little tense.

Mazeery told his brother all he learned about himself and his people as well as his vision from the great lord Nag, however these claims only infuriated his brother who was not afraid of a Negarza Nag when his Egyian people believed in many great Nags.

Mazeery knew if he could not convince his brother to free the Negarza then Nazeerah would destroy the Egyian people, so he begged

Nazeerah on his brothers behalf to be merciful to the Egyians for they had shown the Negarza kindness as well as Xlevary, however this plea fell on deaf ears for Nazeerah knew all to well that Xlevary wasn't the only station in life for Negarza in Egyah, in fact more Negarza lived normal lives, owning businesses and even holding positions of royalty and esteem, but this only angered Nazeerah who believed even one Negarza Xleva was one to many and a direct insult to his glory.

Verse 55

Division separated the Negarza, its the only way a person could see there people in bondage yet do nothing, Nazeerah a Nag of war could never allow his people to look so weak, he would rather wipe the Negarza people from existence than allow them to live in shame, this is why Mazeery needed to change Pharoshems mind.

Verse 56

The Egyians weren't without protection of their own, they were chosen by a group of old, wise and powerful Nags from great klans, that chose

Egyah to be their land of
worship and the Egyians to
be their worshipers, this
made it impossible for
Nazeerah to just carelessly
attack the Egyians, for that
would mean a war between
Nazeerah and the Egyian
Nags.

Seven plagues, this would be
a compromise to avoid war
within the heavens, Nazeerah
would curse his own people,
damming the Negarza to be a
people of victory, their
success would bring riches,
prosperity and peace to the

world, but their failure would bring plagues on any nation in which they are suffering.

Verse 58

The first plague would be drought, for water is the life blood of all living things and so it shall be the first thing taken by the curse of the Negarza, Nazeerahs wrath would cause waters in rivers and lakes to evaporate and vanish, rains to cease, lands to dry up and crops to die, cities would become deserts and people would desiccate.

Verse 59

The second plague would be
scavengers, without crops or
water livestock would began
to die off, the scent of death
bringing vultures, rodents
and jackals who would not
only eat the dead but prey
upon the dying cattle as well,
their hunger being driven by
Nazeerahs hunger for his
peoples freedom.

Verse 60

The third plague would be
infestation, rotten flesh would
bring maggots and flies,
mosquitos and ticks, parasites
would spread and the filth
would match Nazeerahs

disgust for how his people suffer.

Verse 61

The fourth plague would be pestilence, filth, starvation, and the spread of sickness through mosquitos, ticks and rodents, people would become breading grounds for disease and their suffering would pale in comparison to Nazeerah watching his people suffer.

Verse 62

The fifth plague would be Vermaya, drawn to the suffering of the dying and mass deaths that would occur

due to the first four plagues,
Vermaya would make their
presence known in order to
harness the corrupted
Nivenity in the land, this
imbalance would cause a rise
in Ven energy which
Vermaya use to worship their
malevolent Nags known as
Xins as well as cast spells,
these creatures who once
were human women now
filled with so much hatred for
humanity, almost as much as
Nazeerahs hatred of seeing
his people as Xleva.
Verse 63

The sixth plague would be Xinners, Xin underlings born from Xins breading with lower level creatures including humans, these Xinners would be a waking nightmare terrorizing their victims before consuming them, but not even they live up to the nightmare of Nazeerah watching the mistreatment of his people.

Verse 64

The seventh plague would be Xin, the first six plagues would terraform the land creating the perfect conditions for a Xin to enter earth, its hunger ravenous millions would die only equaling a single bite let alone a meal to a Xin, this devastation reminiscent of how devastated Nazeerah feels seeing his people disrespected.

Verse 65

In the end Pharoshem lasted four plagues, by the fourth his people were in shambles and he knew if he held out any longer the damage done would be irreversible, he told his brother to take his people and go, and never return, so Mazeery gathered his people and began an exodus that would shape history.

Seven hundred years would be the duration of the Negarzas journey, in their nomadic travels generations would live and die, Xleva would learn to be free men and free men would learn to be warriors, leaders would spring up and Krowlocks would be born, and before the world knew it, the Negarza were a force to be reckoned with, there were only fourteen Krowmandments Nazeerahs people needed to follow given to Mazeery by one of Nazeerahs kounts.

Verse 67

The Krowmandments were as followed,

1. Pride is power, a person without pride is already dead.

2. War is natural because nature is violent, a person afraid of war isn't fit for survival.

3. Loyalty to your people is how you show love to the great lord Nag, because Nazeerah loves his people.

4. Bringing harm to ones own people is a prayer for Nazeerahs wrath against you.

5. Respect your people as you respect yourself.

6. Victory should always be the goal to any endeavor.

7. Women are to be protected for they are the beauty of peace opposite the ugliness of war.

8. Children are an extension of their parents, to abandon a

child is to live a life without pride.

9. Cowards chose xlavery, the proud should always choose death as opposed to bondage.

10. Knowledge is power, ignorance is the first step towards xlavery.

11. Leaders are to be chosen by the people they lead and no other way.

12. Always strive for physical, mental and spiritual excellence.

13. Fear is and obstacle to overcome and nothing more, even death is only a transition so there is nothing to fear.

14. Your nation is your people, your people are your bloodline, your bloodline is your family, treat every Negarza as you treat your family.

Verse 68

Despite Nazeerah rescuing his people from Xlavery, the Negarza were still hardheaded and foolish children, it wouldn't be long

before they were worshiping
other Nags and taking on the
customs of other nations, and
for this Nazeerah would
punish his children by
turning his back on them
leaving them as sheep among
wolves.
Verse 69

Xleva, or forced servants one
minute, and Krowlocks or
rulers of nations the next, the
Negarza were always either
in power or in servitude,
some would live gloriously
while honoring their great
lord Nag, while others
foolishly worshiped other

Nags or simply turned their backs on their great lord Nag, and unto them curses were placed by their great lord Nag so they may know his wrath and repent and come back into his grace, this disrespect infuriated a lot of Nazeerahs Kounts who believed mankind was undeserving of Nazeerahs time and devotion, so they rebelled against Nazeerah hellbent on destroying the earth and putting and end to mankind, this rebellion would be lead by Legulas the golden light bearer, the most adored and respected of all of Nazeerahs Kounts, the war between the fallen Kounts and the just went on for centuries, both sides losing many Kounts, until the mighty Nikaiel faced off against his fallen brother Legulas and defeated him in combat only sparring his life on orders from Nazeerah himself, instead of death Legulas would receive a punishment far worse than death, banishment to a hell spore, unlike the fruit of the heavens or the flowers of the earths, hell spores are barren wastelands void of NiVen and Disconnected from NiziN, these worlds only exist to maintain the balance, for if worlds capable of creating life exist then worlds designed to take life must exist as well, hell spores feed on any NiVen or Nivenity that ends up on its surface trapping the victims until they cease to exist, for and immortal, damnation to a hell spore means and eternity being fed on unable to escape or even be freed, the only form of salvation would be to give in and allow the hell spore to fully consume you and cease to be, although most of the Kounts of Legulas were banished with him to a hell spore, some were able to escape to earth to hide vowing to one day free their fallen leader.

Verse 70

Throughout history there have been mortals who have possessed an above average amount of Nivenity by mortal standards granting them abilities beyond normal mortal ability, and due to Nags passing on their seed to mortal woman or female

Nags receiving the seed of mortal men, there would be mortals born who's abilities seemed to rival the Nags themselves, it was because of this that Nazeerah had an idea on how he could get the Negarza on the right path by giving them a Krowlock of his own seed, and so he took a young virgin girl of the Negarza nation and into her he planted his seed which would grow and be born in only fourteen days, and on that fourteenth day a boy of both mortal and immortal blood, both man and Nag,

was born, and his name
would be Nyarah the son of
the great lord Nag.
Verse 71

Nyarah, although born from
the seed of a Nag he was still
a boy born into the world of
men, whom had their own
Krowlocks and dominions,
nations, religions and Nags,
which made Nyarah a threat
from birth, great knowa
foretold of the birth of
Nyarah for he was destined to
bring about a great change in
the world, news of this caused
Krowlocks the world over to
call for the boys head, which

caused Nyarahs mother Afrodisces to take her child and flea.

The world is made up of seven continents, the ring of ice known as Vikrendor, a frozen landscape of ice and rock stretching for thousands of miles and incasing the other six continents, Negamureno in the north west, Kastigma in the south west, Euphrea and Tankue in the north east, Kushemett in the southern middle east and Kremenalle in the south east, these continents and the many islands that surround them make up the realm of man, and not to many places were safe for young Nyarah within the realm of man.

Verse 73

Born in Kushemett, Nyarah would flea with his mother Afrodisces into Negamureno where he would be taught the history of his peoples trials and tribulations in Kushemett as well as learn the ways of his peoples who long ago migrated to and conquered the lands of Negamureno.

Nyarah grew in Negamureno learning the cultures and customs of many tribes as well as listening to his mothers stories about his ancestors back in Kushemett, she told tales of great Knowa that foretold of floods and calamities as well as Knowa whom directly spoke to the great lord Nag, she told stories of mythical creatures and great beast as well as tales of mighty Negarza warriors and heroes, and through these tales Nyarah learned of the ways of his people, and vowed to restore his peoples great name.

Verse 75

As Nyarah grew so did his popularity and influence, before long people were coming from all over to hear him speak and he spread the word of Brewl to all of his lost brethren in Negamureno, however it wasn't long till he felt it was time to go and spread Nazeerahs word to those who truly needed it back in Kushemett.

Verse 76

Nyarah now a wise and fierce warrior, returned to

Kushemett to claim his seat as Krowlock of his people, along his journey he would acquire fourteen students who would follow him and chronicle his journey and teachings, he would pass on the history of their ancestors and teach them the laws of their great lord Nag, and over time they would learn the ways of being upright righteous Negarza men.

Verse 76

News of Nyarahs influence reached Krodaminions far and wide and Krowlocks the world over were not pleased, especially the great Krowlock of Shemeeria one of the most powerful nations in Kushemett, his name was both praised and feared, for Golamaaris the golden calf was known for his cunning and victory in battle, and he who believed himself to be of divine descent could not allow another to spread falsehoods of being the son of a Nag.

Verse 77

Nyarah was know fool, he knew his very existence was a threat to any Krowlocks reign, for what would be the purpose of any man bending a knee to another man when they could be led by the son of a Nag, thus he came prepared for war because his Nag was a Nag of war and worshipers of his Nag are men and women of war.

Verse 78

Over the next few years Nyarah and his band of brothers would see many battles and before they knew it they were a small army leading a rebellion against the evils of the world, evils perpetrated by Legalia, the oldest cult known to man, originally formed by outcast banished from the NiJaBre klan, over hundreds of millennia Legalia has formed many cults in order to hide and insulate themselves from discovery, their main goal to corrupt worlds and Inxleva all who oppose them.

Verse 79

Legalia was in control of every major government, civilization was their greatest weapon and the law their noose around the necks of the masses, knowing this Nyarah took up arms against the government itself making him and his followers the enemies of the world.

Nyarah was branded a criminal, his supposed crime was blasphemy, with the church, the government and political puppets like Golamaaris under their thumb Legalia had the deck stacked in their favor, a war against the whole world would be foolish so Nyarah devised a plan that would ensure his people and his teachings would live on, he would become a martyr, a symbol of rebellion and faith

in the teachings of the true
lord Nag, his fourteen Kounts
including the one who
betrayed him would serve a
purpose in bringing his words
to the world for a millennia
to come, and one day those
words would inspire an army
to rise up against the evils of
Legalia and free the world
from their grip.

Verse 81

The trial was swift, Nyarah
was found guilty and
sentenced to death, for
fourteen days he endured
cruelty and torture far worse
than anything imaginable in

hopes his spirit would be broken and Legalia could convince him to admit to the world his Nag was a false Nag and he was a blasphemer, but he never gave in and kept his head held high and his pride intact, and on the day he was to be executed thunder and lightening filled the air as rain fell from the heavens as if the world itself was weeping, and as his son prepared for death Nazeerah looked on knowing his intervention would only sully his sons honor as a warrior, and as per tradition he was Kruzafide, a tradition

that got its name from a
fierce Jekon, a race of beings
known for
being twice, to a hundred
times larger than normal men
and women, Kroxce the
Kruzafier was his name and
he was known for leaving the
bodies of slaughtered men
and women on Jekon swords
like diced lamb on a skewer,
after his defeat by a Negarza
boy named Dulteer who
would one day be a
Krowlock, the tradition was
started to pay tribute to
Dulteer, and so Nyarahs wrist
and feet were nailed to a

Jekon sized wooden sword Kruzafix, and on that Kroxce he died with a smile on his face knowing one day he would rise again.

Nyarahs death sent shockwaves through the world, the spark of rebellion was ignited in the hearts of many, including members of the NiJaBre klan who realized they had allowed Legalia to grow too powerful, the majority of the klan decided to remain neutral but those who decided to leave their klan created a secret society known as Kolt with one major goal, to destroy Legalia and all their minions.

Verse 83

Nyarahs Kounts would each set out on solitary journeys each in their own way spreading the knowledge they gained while at Nyarahs side, Kolt would continue their unseen war against Legalia in the shadows and civilizations would continue to rise and fall until the day of Xkardem, a word like no other for no one knows its true origin, engraved on a golden Krown before the title of Krowlock existed and found by the NiJaBre people within a volcano before any other nations existed, it was merely and unknown, many believed it to have come from the Nags, but not even the oldest Nags knew what the engraved word meant, knowa throughout history wrote about great battles in the distant future and hellish scenes that led some to believe a war of wars was looming in the distance and the Krown was a warning, however only one being knew

for sure, the child of
prophecy, and he knew
Xkardem meant the end of
existence.

Verse 84

Fourteen Kounts of Nyarah,
each would spread his word
after his death from their own
perspective, their names
would be carved into legend,
Agreshion the ember,
Tuskornivo the just, Grayle
the shadow, Cryear the heart,
Lepara the fearless, Vyonis
the kloth, Lukyle the strict,
Skallios the free, Shigero the
unwavering, Cajah the
teacher, Atix the healer,

Pressheous the artist, Belosa the traitor, and Ghostian the great, these Kounts would create fourteen different belief systems that would lay the foundation for modern civilization.

Verse 85

Agreshion the ember, born in Vikrendor he grew up in a world where everyday was a struggle for survival this is what drew him to Nyarahs tales of a war Nag that rewarded the strong and the brave, in Agreshions teachings he would spread the gospel of war and unify

an army under the name of
Nyarah known as the church
of Sentimon, named after one
of Nazeerahs great warrior
Kounts, it would be the belief
of followers of the church of
Sentimon that true peace can
only come from victory in
war.

Verse 86

Tuskornivo the just, born in
Kushemett young
Tuskornivo knew both peace
and prosperity, it was
Nyarahs teachings about
unity and peace that lead him
to establishing the church of
Kongoa, named after

Nazeerahs most trusted adviser and council, it is believed by the followers of the church of Kongoa that peace is the primary goal of life and that peace must be defended with ones life if necessary.

Verse 87

Grayle the shadow, born in Kremenalle was surrounded by liars and cheats, a world where even the swindlers get swindled, what drew him to Nyarah was his honesty, Nyarah never painted his great lord Nag as Perfect, his Nag was fierce and violent, caring and compassionate, proud and jealous, these different conflicting emotions humanized Nazeerah in the eyes of Grayle which made him feel more connected to him, Grayle would establish the church of Akara, named after a Nag that gave Nazeerah his only defeat in his youth as well as a Scar on his eye that served as a reminder of his past weakness, Nazeerah would grow and never taste defeat again only to face off with Akara in the future and defeat him, but even in defeating Akara he spared him and recruited him into his army, followers of the church of Akara believe in redemption, growth and forgiveness.

Verse 88

Cryear the heart, born on an island off the koast of Negamureno, Cryear was raised to value community and family for his people were a tribal people, it was Nyarahs teachings of the bloodline of the Negarza that drew Cryear in, he would go on to establish the church of Karihada, named after the

Kount chosen by Nazeerah to watch over the Negarza people during their journey out of Egyah, followers of Karihada strive to unify the bloodline of the Negarza.

Verse 89

Lepara the fearless, born in Kushemett to a noble family he was drawn in by Nyarahs teachings on the earth being the kingdom of the Negarza by birthright, he would establish the church of Godrah, named after Nazeerahs father who died in battle while Nazeerah was still a young child, followers

of the church of Godrah
believe the world is their
birthright and uphold victory
above all else.

Vyonis the kloth, born in
Egyah he knew hatred,
growing up a Negarza klan
member in a world with so
much animosity against the
Negarza he was drawn to
Nyarahs pride in being
Negarzian, he would go on to
establish the church of
Fallazede, named after the
kount Nazeerah chose to find
him a people worthy of
worshiping him, it was

Fallazede that found the Negarza, a people descended from the NiJaBre, followers of the church of Fallazede believe knowledge of self will unify and bring peace to the world.

Verse 91

Lukyle the strict, born in Tankue he was raised to value tradition and law, it was Nyarahs teachings of the Krowmandments that Lukyle was inspired by, he would go on to establish the church of Vazzo, named after the kount Nazeerah sent to bring Mazeery the

Krowmandments, followers of the church of Vazzo believe rules and structure given to them within the Krowmandments are the key to peace and prosperity.

Verse 92

Skallios the free, born in Kastigma to a tribal people freedom meant everything to Skallios which is why when he heard Nyarah teaching about freedom at all cost he was entranced, he would go on to establish the church of Borchellos a young spirited kount Nazeerah sees as a younger brother figure, followers of the church of Borchellos value freedom in every aspect and shun civilization fearing its only purpose is to steal peoples freedoms.

Verse 93

Shigero the unwavering, born in Euphrea, class and hierarchy was everything and as a Negarza Shigero and his people were on the bottom, for this reason he was drawn to Nyarahs teachings and felt they would uplift his people, he would go on to establish the church of Hejaku, named after one of Nazeerahs kounts who discovered what Legulas was plotting and tried to stop him and his rebels single handed only to be killed in battle by the fallen kounts of Legulas, followers of the church of Hejaku believe faith and loyalty are worth dying for.

Verse 94

Cajah the teacher, born in Vikrendor where most men valued brute force, Cajah believed knowledge was true power, it was Nyarahs teachings about Nyince that captivated him, he would go on to establish the church of

Nyleon, named after the most intelligent of all of Nazeerahs kounts, followers of the church of Nyleon believe knowledge to be the greatest form of empowerment.

Verse 95

Atix the healer, born in Negamureno Atix was raised to be a Papalito a healer who uses the power of NiVen for the good of the world, his mother a Mayalita which is a female Papalito was killed by Vermaya when Atix was a child, he vowed to vanquish evil from the world which is why Nyarahs teachings about

Nivenity and its uses
intrigued Atix, he would go
on to establish the church of
Lubelle, named after one of
the fiercest of Nazeerahs
kounts who earned the name
Xin eater by single handedly
slaughtering a thousands
Xins in one of his most
glorious battles, followers of
the church of Lubelle believe
it is their sworn duty to
remove evil from the world.

Verse 96

Pressheous the artist, born on
an island off the koast of
Kremenalle young
Pressheous was a free spirit

who saw the beauty in the world and loved nature, it was Nyarahs teachings about the balance of the natural and spiritual world that Pressheous gravitated to, he would go on to establish the church of Jinero, named after Nazeerahs kount who was chosen to be a guardian on earth, followers of the church of Jinero believe it is their duty to protect and be one with nature.

Verse 97

Belosa the traitor, born in Euphrea Belosa was always a coward, Nyarahs bravery is what inspired him but in the end he would betray Nyarah in exchange for his own freedom and six gold coins, giving his enemies information about Nyarahs location they were able to capture him, Belosa would go on to establish the church of Sedeneve, named after Nazeerahs arch nemesis and one of the oldest Xins, followers of the church of Sedeneve believe their own pleasure is all that matters and want to watch the world burn.

Verse 98

Ghostian the great, born in Negamureno into a warrior tribe Ghostian was born for battle after hearing Nyarah speak of great battles taking place in the heavens and future wars coming to earth he desired nothing more than to fight for Nazeerah in a glorious battle, he would establish the church of Stormear, named after the kount of prophecy said to walk the earth on the day of Oblitherance, where Nazeerahs kounts and the Xins lead by Sedeneve would do battle on earth, followers

of the church of Stormear
believe life is merely
preparation for one day
fighting along side Nazeerah
in his army.

Verse 99
Brewl, pieced together by
scholars using all the known
pages of Brewl in existence
this is more than incomplete
to say the least, Brewl is
infinite, never ending and
forever changing, let it serve
as a guide to understanding
something truly
inconceivable, what you
knew about religion was

wrong, what you knew about history was wrong, what you thought was science was wrong, even the natural world was skewed for your ignorance, you were a fool but by now you know some small truths, there are many lost pages of Brewl, you may seek them out but if you find them…

www.ingramcontent.com/pod-product-compliance
Lightning Source LLC
Chambersburg PA
CBHW050413030726
47503CB00006B/2164